# THE BOY WHO SPOKE TO THE EARTH

CHRIS BURKARD - DAVID McCLELLAN

Text copyright © 2015 by Chris Burkard. Illustrations copyright © 2015 by David McClellan. Published by Dreamling Books.

Special thanks to Designer: Piper Morgan. Art Director: Jesse Draper. Editor: Alex Masterson. Dreamling Books is devoted

to sharing uplifting and inspiring stories. We all have a story to tell. Share yours at www.dreamlingbooks.com. All rights

reserved. Library of Congress Control Number: 2014947312. ISBN: 978-0-9800123-3-0. Printed in China.

18  19  20     10  9  8  7  6  5

SALT LAKE CITY

For my two sons, Jeremiah and
Forrest. I hope this book serves as a
guide for all the exploring that
awaits you... Of all of my adventures,
the greatest were you two. — CB

For Erin, Brian, Matthew, Nathan,
and Connor. And for everyone who
likes oceans, cliffs, forests, deserts,
and mountains. — DM

THERE ONCE

WAS A BOY

WHO SPOKE

TO THE

EARTH

... AND THE EARTH
SPOKE BACK.

"EARTH, ARE YOU LISTENING?"

"MY BOY, I AM
**ALWAYS** LISTENING."

" WHERE CAN I FIND

HAPPINESS ? "

" THE JOURNEY TO

# HAPPINESS

IS DIFFICULT, BUT I CAN SHOW YOU THE WAY,"

SAID THE EARTH.


"ARE YOU WILLING TO MAKE THE JOURNEY?"


"OH, I AM," SAID THE BOY.

AND HE MEANT IT.

"THEN GO TO
**THE OCEAN,**
WHERE WAVES
TOWER OVERHEAD,"

SAID THE EARTH.

SO THE BOY BEGAN TO WALK.

"I SEE THE WATER AND THE SHELLS," SAID THE BOY.

"BUT I DON'T SEE HAPPINESS."

" THEN GO TO

# THE CLIFFS,

WHERE WATER IS

ALWAYS FLOWING,"

SAID THE EARTH.

SO THE BOY WADED AND HE WANDERED
UNTIL HE LEFT THE WAVES BEHIND.

"I SEE THE **SPRAY AND THE MOSS**," SAID THE BOY.

"BUT I DON'T
SEE HAPPINESS."

"THEN GO TO

# THE FOREST,

WHERE TREES
GATHER TOGETHER,"

SAID THE EARTH.

SO THE BOY STEPPED AND HE STRODE
UNTIL HE LEFT THE MOSS BEHIND.

"I SEE THE ROOTS AND THE LEAVES," SAID THE BOY.

"BUT I DON'T
SEE HAPPINESS."

"THEN GO TO

# THE DESERT,

WHERE RED STONE

GUARDS THE WAY,"

SAID THE EARTH.

SO THE BOY HIKED AND HE HAULED
UNTIL HE LEFT THE TREES BEHIND.

"I SEE THE **SAND AND THE STONE**," SAID THE BOY.

"BUT I DON'T SEE HAPPINESS."

" THEN GO TO

# THE MOUNTAINS,

WHERE PEAKS TOUCH

THE CLOUDS,"

SAID THE EARTH.

SO THE BOY TREKKED AND HE TRUDGED
UNTIL HE LEFT THE SAND BEHIND.

"I SEE THE **ROCKS AND THE BRUSH**," SAID THE BOY.

"BUT I DON'T SEE HAPPINESS."

" THEN GO TO
# THE TOP <sub>OF</sub> <sub>THE</sub> WORLD,
WHERE LIGHTS DANCE
IN THE SKY, "

SAID THE EARTH.


SO THE BOY CLIMBED AND HE CRAWLED
UNTIL HE LEFT THE PEAKS BEHIND.

"I SEE THE **ICE AND THE SNOW,**" SAID THE BOY.

"BUT I DON'T SEE HAPPINESS."

THIS TIME, THE EARTH DIDN'T ANSWER.

SO THE BOY WALKED

AND HE WALKED

AND HE WALKED

UNTIL HE LEFT IT ALL BEHIND.

" I'VE TRAVELED SO FAR AND SEEN SO MUCH,
BUT I **STILL** HAVEN'T FOUND HAPPINESS."

"EARTH, ARE YOU LISTENING?"

CRIED THE BOY.

# "MY BOY,

DID YOU LOOK

WITHOUT

## SEEING?"

ASKED THE EARTH.

"GO BACK ALONG THE TRAIL, BUT THIS TIME,
STAND STILL FOR JUST A MOMENT."

SO HE WENT BACK AND LOOKED AGAIN.

AND FOR THE FIRST TIME, THE BOY

## TRULY SAW ...

# HAPPINESS

WAS ALL AROUND HIM.